Jona

The Secret Life of SQUIRRELS
BACK TO SCHOOL!

Nancy Rose

Megan Tingley Books

LITTLE, BROWN AND COMPANY
NEW YORK   BOSTON

Most squirrels spend the last days of summer preparing for the cold. Not Mr. Peanuts and Rosie! They have a bigger job to do.

School starts tomorrow, and Rosie needs to get her classroom ready. She is very excited. (And also a little nervous.)

Mr. Peanuts chirps, "Let's go back-to-school shopping, Rosie."

Good idea, Mr. Peanuts!

They head to the store. Rosie fills her cart with notebooks and paper, paints, and crayons.

"I love buying school supplies," she tells Mr. Peanuts. "It's just as much fun as gathering nuts!"

There is so much to do before Rosie's students arrive. First, Mr. Peanuts helps her unpack all the books. He knows every classroom needs a great library.

Rosie hangs a big banner on the wall.
She wants all her students to feel welcome.

Then she posts the class rules on the bulletin board. Rosie knows that these will help everyone start the year off on the right paw. Her favorite rule is *Listen while others are speaking.* Can you imagine if all those little squirrels chattered at the same time?

Mr. Peanuts is outside helping clean the field when he spots some sports equipment. "These look like fun!" he exclaims. Mr. Peanuts quite likes to play basketball.

"Yes, the students will really enjoy recess and gym class with these," says Mr. Chipper, the gym teacher. "Thank you for helping me with them!"

Mr. Peanuts goes back inside, to find Rosie organizing craft supplies. "Can you help me set up the art corner, Mr. Peanuts?"

Mr. Peanuts starts to move a table, but he pushes too hard and the purple paint can tips over!

"Not to worry," Rosie says, smiling. "Accidents happen." Rosie is a very kind teacher. (And she always makes sure there are *lots* of paper towels.)

Mr. Peanuts spots a guitar in the corner and starts to play. "You should join my class for a sing-along one day!" says Rosie. "It would be such a treat."

"I would be happy to," says Mr. Peanuts. He is a really talented musician. Rosie is, too! She plays the xylophone beautifully. She likes to teach "I Had a Little Nut Tree" to the young squirrels.

After all that work, their stomachs are grumbling. Time for lunch! Mr. Peanuts and Rosie head outside to find a picnic table in a nice shady spot.

"The playground won't be quiet for long," Rosie says. "It will be full of happy chatter tomorrow."

After lunch, Mr. Peanuts says, "I'm going to drive the bus route, so I'd better practice!" He makes double sure he knows where all the new students live. Wait, Mr. Peanuts! That's not how you steer the bus! Is that how you watch for traffic?

Meanwhile, Rosie tidies up the community garden. Burrowing into the ground is a lot of hard work! What seeds should she buy for the students to plant this year?

Rosie gets back to rearranging her classroom and unpacking boxes. She finds her first-aid kit and an extra box of bandages and stores them in the closet. *These will come in handy if someone gets their tail in a knot,* she thinks.

Suddenly, Rosie hears a friendly voice. She peeks into the classroom across the hall and sees Miss Chattery at her desk. Rosie stops in to say hello.

Then Rosie goes to the big hall to make sure everything is ready for the welcome address. She has a great speech prepared! "Testing, testing. Is this thing on?" she says into the microphone. Mr. Peanuts gives her a thumbs-up from the back!

Sunnywood
Education
Center

In her classroom, Rosie finishes her lesson plan. *We will start the day reading the Nutshell Library,* she thinks. They are some of her favorite books.

Rosie wants the first day of school to be just perfect. She checks her list. All done!

Tomorrow will be the best first day ever, Rosie thinks.
And it will be!

About This Book

The Secret Life of Squirrels: Back to School! and the other titles in the series—*The Secret Life of Squirrels, Merry Christmas, Squirrels!*, and *The Secret Life of Squirrels: A Love Story*—were inspired by the busy and inquisitive squirrels in Nancy Rose's backyard in Canada. When these squirrels became regular visitors to Nancy's bird feeders, she began taking photographs of them and eventually added miniature handmade sets for fun. She creates the sets, positions them on her deck, and watches through the glass door for the squirrels' approach. Her camera is on a tripod by the door so that she can capture the squirrels in action. She makes most of her own props, such as the school bus, classroom furniture, playground equipment, podium, and little blue backpack that appear in this book, and occasionally uses some existing miniature items, such as the music equipment and baskets, to decorate her sets. These days, Nancy's friends, old and new, offer her little things to use in her sets, with some, like the shopping cart, coming from as far away as Germany.

Amazingly, she does not manipulate the photographs digitally to position the squirrels in the scenes—she gets the squirrels to pose by hiding peanuts in and around the props. Nancy enjoys photographing squirrels in particular because she loves their curiosity. It's also challenging to photograph them—they move very quickly. Sometimes it can take more than a hundred shots to get just the right image!

This book was edited by Megan Tingley and Mary-Kate Gaudet and designed by Whitney Manger with art direction by Jen Keenan. The production was supervised by Erika Schwartz, and the production editor was Jen Graham. The text was set in Berliner, and the display type is Woodrow. The photographs in this book, including the squirrels and the textured backgrounds, were taken using a Canon 6D, with various lenses, such as the Canon 70-200mm, Canon 24-105mm, and Canon 100-400mm.

Little, Brown and Company
Hachette Book Group
1290 Avenue of the Americas, New York, NY 10104
Visit us at LBYR.com

First Edition: July 2018

Little, Brown and Company is a division of Hachette Book Group, Inc.
The Little, Brown name and logo are trademarks of Hachette Book Group, Inc.

The publisher is not responsible for websites (or their content) that are not owned by the publisher.

Library of Congress Cataloging-in-Publication Data
Names: Rose, Nancy (Nancy Patricia), 1954– author, illustrator.
Title: The secret life of squirrels : back to school! / Nancy Rose.
Other titles: Back to school!
Description: First edition. | New York ; Boston : Little, Brown and Company, 2018. | "Megan Tingley Books." | Summary: As summer comes to an end, Mr. Peanuts helps his friend, Rosie, prepare her classroom and the school for the students' return.
Identifiers: LCCN 2017032894| ISBN 9780316506212 (hardcover) | ISBN 9780316506199 (ebook library edition) | ISBN 9780316506182 (ebook fixed format)
Subjects: | CYAC: Teachers—Fiction. | Schools—Fiction. | First day of school—Fiction. | Squirrels—Fiction.
Classification: LCC PZ7.R717813 Sj 2018 | DDC [E]—dc23
LC record available at https://lccn.loc.gov/2017032894

ISBNs: 978-0-316-50621-2 (hardcover), 978-0-316-50618-2 (ebook), 978-0-316-50616-8 (ebook), 978-0-316-50620-5 (ebook)

10 9 8 7 6 5 4 3 2 1

APS

Printed in China

Photo credits: Jacket front flap and spine (crayons): Yellow Cat/Shutterstock.com • Jacket flaps, back cover, 26 (ruler): Quang Ho/Shutterstock.com • Jacket front flap, 5, 27 (paper texture): Taigi/Shutterstock.com • Jacket back cover, 1, 14, 27, 32 (chalkboard): kckate16/Shutterstock.com • Jacket back cover, 31 (pushpins): FabrikaSimf/Shutterstock.com • Jacket back cover, 28, 32 (pencil): Ruslan Ivantsov/Shutterstock.com • 5 (twig frame): Basileus/Shutterstock.com • 11 (striped cloth): siro46/Shutterstock.com • 19 (apples): ilaszlo/Shutterstock.com • 24, 30 (paper clips): Robbi/Shutterstock.com